LOUIE!

Will Hillenbrand

PHILOMEL BOOKS

Dear Ludwig Bemelmans,

To you and Madeline I have dedicated this book. My life has been made better

because of you. No person can give to the next generation what it does not have.

You, the alchemist, gave us gold.　　—WH

nce upon a time there lived a little pig named Louie.
He loved warm sunny days, sticky mud, the lilting
songs of birds, and drawing.

He also loved the stories his mother would tell him of her own piglethood. How she had been small and a little mischievous. How she had been sent to an old schoolhouse in Paris that was covered in vines, where the girls walked in two straight lines.

Louie would stay up late and draw parts of her story.

Louie started school.

While all of the other pigs worked on
their lessons, Louie drew pictures of
the things that made him happy.

Soon, classmates giggled, calling Louie, "Potato head! *Tête de linotte!*
Tête en l'air!"

He was so miserable, he didn't even want to draw.

So Louie was sent to another school. A school that promised to pass "even the dullest of pigs."

Louie tried—he read stories and answered the teacher's questions—but in the margins of his papers, he drew pictures of things that made him happy.

The headmaster sent him home for good. *"Petit porc stupide!"* he said.

Desperate, Louie's mother sent him to his uncle and aunt who owned a hotel. "You'll help them, and they will help you, Little Louie," his mother said hopefully.

"Welcome, Louie," said his uncle and aunt. They gave Louie
a grand tour all around the hotel, ending at his little room.
 Louie went right to work, vacuuming,
scrubbing dirty dishes, dusting,
lugging heavy bags . . .

and drawing pictures on windows before washing them.

On his birthday Louie received a set of brightly colored crayons, sketching pencils and a drawing journal from his aunt and uncle.

Keeping his journal with him, now Louie drew and drew and drew, until the journal was filled with sketches.

One evening an uppity odd-looking couple came to the hotel. Louie slipped behind a potted palm. Hmmmmm, they would be fun to draw, thought Louie. Picking up a nearby menu, he drew on the back side of it.

Unknowingly, the headwaiter snatched the menus from Louie
and handed them to the uppity odd-looking couple.

"*Qu'est-ce que c'est? Un outrage!*" said the uppity old man.

"We'll sue," said the old woman.

Louie knew he would be sent home once again.

Waving drawings of the uppity couple, Louie's uncle and aunt found him packing his bags. "Wait!" said his aunt. "These drawings are good!"

"My friend Vincent buys art for pigs all over the world!" said his uncle. "Unpack your things, Louie . . . my friend wants to look at all of your drawings tomorrow."

And, yes, Vincent who bought art for pigs all over the world loved Louie's drawings. But he said, "Why not draw little pigs like yourself?"

"GREAT idea," said Louie. That would definitely make him happy.

Years passed. Louie still worked at the hotel drawing pictures. He drew banker pigs, cook pigs, mama and papa pigs, uncle pigs, and many, many little pigs. Some of his drawings of big and little pigs were so good, they were put on the covers of magazines!

He met a fine lady, Miss May. She wore a very large hat and she was an editor. She made books for little piggies! "I want to see every pig you've ever drawn," she declared.

He showed her every picture he'd ever drawn in his journal, on menus, even some drawings on his window blinds (he had run out of paper again).

Miss May said, "Oooh la la, Louie, you should draw books for little piggies."

"GREAT idea," said Louie. He was happy just thinking about it.

In the spring, when delivering a new drawing to a magazine company, Louie met a girl. Her name was Mimi and she wanted to become a model.

"Oh, Mimi," Louie said, "you are as pretty as a picture." And of course he meant it.

They soon married right there in Paris.

Tragically, on their honeymoon, while Louie and Mimi were bicycling, poor Louie was thrown from his bicycle by a speeding car.

"Louie," Mimi cried. "My Louie!"

Louie was rushed to the hospital, where he spent many days getting better.

"This is some honeymoon," Louie grumped. How he missed Mimi.

While convalescing, Louie heard something in the next room. It was a mischievous young girl who had just had her appendix removed.

"It's the girl!" Louie said. "It's the right girl." And he pulled out his journal and started to draw.

The little girl reminded Louie of his mother and her stories—of the convent school, the little beds all in a row, little girls all dressed alike, and a little girl smaller and more mischievous than the others.

He started drawing—then writing. "In an old house in Paris that was covered with vines . . . "

He could hardly wait to show Mimi.

Mimi loved it.

Soon the story was published in a book, a book by that very editor with the big hat! It brought joy to millions of little piggies. They loved the mischievous little girl, the beds in rows and how the girls walked in two straight lines.

This launched Louie into a lifetime of success. He lived his remaining days making pictures and delighting little and medium-sized and big piggies everywhere.

And this made him very, very happy.

A Note from Will Hillenbrand

Louie! is most truly a story about an artist, for very often the artist's life takes a different path from that of a great many other people. At the same time, I was intrigued with a particular artist, Ludwig Bemelmans, the creator of *Madeline*, and so I based this story very loosely on his life.

Ludwig himself was born in Austria, and indeed his mother often told him stories about her childhood at a boarding school that was "covered with vines" and about the girls who "walked in two straight lines." Unlike Louie, Ludwig's father left the family when he was very young. Ludwig constantly had difficulty in school and was later apprenticed to his uncle Hans at a hotel, but he eventually migrated to the United States, where he spent years working at hotels and restaurants. Like many young Americans at the time, he joined the U.S. Army and became an officer, but he never stopped drawing.

It was when he met May Massee, a children's book editor at Viking, that his career as an illustrator blossomed, beginning with *Hansi* in 1934. Bemelmans did have a serious bicycle accident and was hospitalized, and while in the hospital, he did notice a crack on the ceiling that, to him, looked like a rabbit. More important, he met a young girl there who showed him the scar from where she had had her appendix removed. Her spunk reminded him of the little girl in his mother's stories, who went to the school that was covered with vines. The result was *Madeline*, which was first published in 1939, and has been beloved by every generation—including fellow artists—ever since.

Ludwig Bemelmans: April 27, 1898–October 1, 1962

Ludwig Bemelmans' life and work has been chronicled
by his grandson, John Bemelmans Marciano, in
BEMELMANS: The Life and Art of Madeline's Creator.

Patricia Lee Gauch, Editor

PHILOMEL BOOKS   A division of Penguin Young Readers Group.   Published by The Penguin Group.
Penguin Group (USA) Inc., 375 Hudson Street, New York, NY 10014, U.S.A.
Penguin Group (Canada), 90 Eglinton Avenue East, Suite 700, Toronto, Ontario M4P 2Y3, Canada (a division of Pearson Penguin Canada Inc.).   Penguin Books Ltd, 80 Strand,
London WC2R 0RL, England.   Penguin Ireland, 25 St. Stephen's Green, Dublin 2, Ireland (a division of Penguin Books Ltd).   Penguin Group (Australia), 250 Camberwell
Road, Camberwell, Victoria 3124, Australia (a division of Pearson Australia Group Pty Ltd).   Penguin Books India Pvt Ltd, 11 Community Centre, Panchsheel Park, New Delhi
- 110 017, India.   Penguin Group (NZ), 67 Apollo Drive, Rosedale, North Shore 0632, New Zealand (a division of Pearson New Zealand Ltd).   Penguin Books (South Africa)
(Pty) Ltd, 24 Sturdee Avenue, Rosebank, Johannesburg 2196, South Africa.   Penguin Books Ltd, Registered Offices: 80 Strand, London WC2R 0RL, England.
Copyright © 2009 by Will Hillenbrand.

The illustrations were done with ink, pencil, finger-paint, collage and gouache on vellum. These elements were scanned, digitally manipulated
and printed on watercolor paper. Final details were added with colored pencil.
Design by Semadar Megged.

APR 14 2009

Library of Congress Cataloging-in-Publication Data
Hillenbrand, Will.   Louie! / by Will Hillenbrand.   p. cm.   Summary: Louie the pig loves to draw but it gets him thrown out of every school he attends, so he goes to live with
his aunt and uncle who help him realize he has a wonderful talent.   [1. Pigs—Fiction. 2. Artists—Fiction. 3. Drawing—Fiction.] I. Title.
PZ7.H55773Lo 2009   [E]—dc22   2008019453
ISBN 978-0-399-24707-1
1 3 5 7 9 10 8 6 4 2

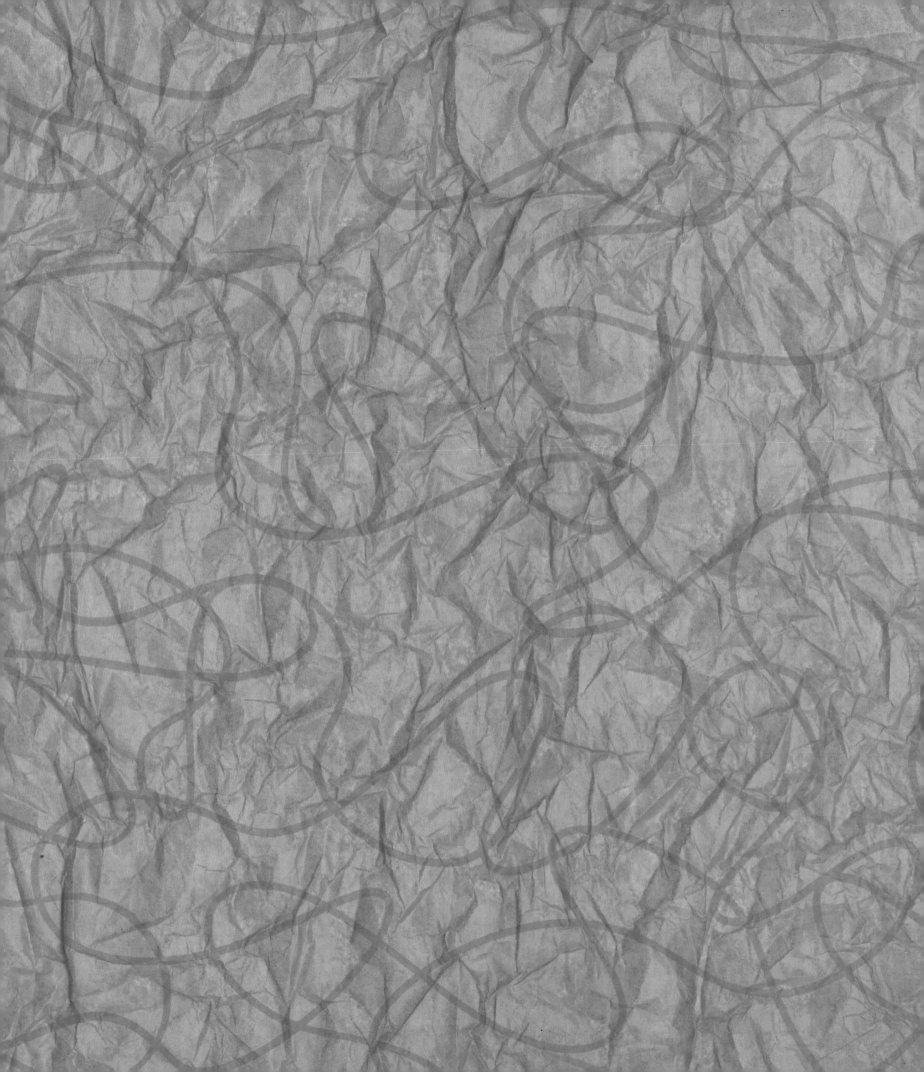